CHESTER THE WORLDLY PIG

Written and illustrated by BILL PEET

HOUGHTON MIFFLIN COMPANY BOSTON

To my wife MARGARET and my sons BILL and STEVE

Library of Congress catalog card number: 65-11023

ISBN: 0-395-18470-3
ISBN: 0-395-27271-8/(pbk.)

Printed in the United States of America

WOZ   30   29   28   27

"OF ALL things," grumbled Chester, "why on earth did I have to be a pig? A pig is no better off than a cabbage or a carrot, just something to eat. But before I end up as so much sausage and ham, I intend to try and amount to something."

But what else could a pig ever be? That was Chester's main problem, and he turned this around and around in his head until one day it suddenly came to him; "I'll be a star in the circus!"

What gave Chester such an outlandish idea was a circus poster which appeared on the barn wall one sunny morning in May. And what caught the little pig's eye was a seal with a ball balanced on the tip of his nose.

"The nose," said Chester, "that's the thing. Surely my flat pig snout must be good for something." And he searched the pigpen for an idea. There was only a trough, a fence, and a mud puddle.

"The trough is much too cumbersome," he decided. "And I can't very well balance a fence or a mud puddle on my nose. So it'll have to work just the other way around. I'll balance my nose on something, on the flat top of a fence post."

Anyone knows that a pig can't climb, but Chester couldn't let this bit of useless knowledge hold him down; and, with a slight boost from an overturned bucket, he struggled up the side of the fence until he was finally perched on the top rail.

Now came the tricky part. Placing his snout squarely on the post, he carefully raised one hind leg in the air, then the other, and with a flurry of short kicks he launched his body up over his head, and for an instant he teetered upside down on his nose. Then down he tumbled to land with a *sploosh!* in the feed trough.

"Well, so far so bad," he muttered; but Chester had no idea of quitting. Before he ever mastered the trick, he expected to take quite a few such tumbles. And indeed he did; he took hundreds of tumbles that day, and by nightfall he was a very weary and badly bruised pig. But, surprisingly enough, his spirits were high. The last effort had been a great improvement; he had held his balance for what he guessed to be a full minute.

And the next morning, after a few more tumbles, Chester had mastered the impossible feat. He could stand on his nose for as long as he pleased, and now he was all set to be discovered. This was no big problem; it had been figured out from the beginning. A railroad ran right past the farm, and the pig was sure that sooner or later the circus train would be coming by there. Whenever he heard a locomotive chugging far down the track, he scrambled up the fence and quickly went into his nose stand. He was always ready just in case.

Then sure enough, early one morning there came the circus train with its long flat cars loaded with animal wagons and tent poles, followed by the elegant red coaches. As the coaches rumbled by, Chester could tell from his upside-down view that all the window shades were drawn. On the train between towns the weary circus people always try to catch up with their sleep, so no one happened to see the pig on the post.

"Oh well," sighed Chester, "it looks like I'll have to take a trip." And he scrambled to the ground outside the fence and set off down the railroad track. It was as simple as that. There was no need to worry about the farmer, for he was always so busy he didn't even know he owned a little spotted pig. And when Chester went trotting by the field where he was plowing, the man merely chuckled. "Well now, it appears to me that somebody's pigpen could stand a little fixin'."

Chester realized that the circus might have gone a long way before stopping to set up the tents—no telling how far. So he settled down to a good steady dogtrot, with his eyes fixed on the track just ahead.

And before he knew it there was the big top, and he stopped with an *oink!* of surprise. This huge mountain of canvas looming above a bustling city of tents and wagons was almost too much for a little farm pig to take all at once, and at first he could only stare in amazement.

Then sternly he warned himself, "If I lose nerve now, I'm through before I start. So if I'm going to be a big star, it's time I got used to big things. The bigger, the better." And with renewed courage he went trotting ahead into the bustling circus lot.

Chester was nimble and quick for a pig, and he managed to dodge and sidestep his way through the army of hustling roustabouts without getting kicked or stepped on. When he came to an open space near the back door of the big top, he picked out a tent stake exactly the right height, and on his very first try went into a perfect nose stand. Then in no time at all Chester was discovered by the circus tall man.

"Hey, everybody!" he shouted. "Look at that little ole pig way

down there!" And suddenly Chester was the center of attention, with
everyone talking at once.

"Say, that's a pretty nifty trick!"

"A real ding-dong doozie!"

"Why he's a natural-born acrobat!"

"Where'd he come from?"

"What's the difference? Let's put him in the show!" And Chester
was hustled away to a dressing tent.

Two attendants tied a red ribbon around his middle, fastened a feathery plume on his head, and gave his precious snout a bit of a shine with a dab of pink shoe polish. And the next thing the little pig knew, he was riding into the big top at the head of the grand parade on a magnificent white stallion led by a beautiful circus queen.

"It just can't be true," thought Chester, tingling with excitement. "This must be a glorious dream. It's much too good to last." And indeed it *was* too good to last; in a very short while the glorious dream turned into more of a nightmare.

For to Chester's horror, when the main show began he found himself in the big cage with five ferocious tigers. Someone had decided the small pig's act must be more spectacular, it needed an element of danger, and the ringmaster's booming voice filled the tent as he announced the spectacular new act.

"Now, for the very first time anywhere, we proudly present Percival, the performing pig! The one and only pig with the dauntless courage and daring ever to perform in the very same arena with savage beasts of the jungle!"

Just as the announcement was finished, the courageous Percival fainted, and he was quickly carried out of the big cage amid a storm of hooting and jeering from the angry spectators.

Chester was quickly revived with a splash of cold lemonade; then he was dressed in baby clothes with a lace bonnet tied under his chin, and Roscoe the clown in a frilly skirt and flowered hat wheeled him around the big top in a doll buggy. A rippling wave of laughter followed after them and someone squealed, "Oh, what a darling adorable little pig!" And after five or six trips around the tent, the poor pig had turned almost the color of the clown's needle nose.

Late that night, after the last performance, Roscoe took off his costume and make-up. Then without so much as one glance at Chester, he turned down the lamp and crawled into bed, leaving the disgruntled pig chained to a tent post and still wearing the miserable bonnet and dress. There was no wriggling out of it, for the ribbon was tied in a double knot under his chin, so he suspected that as long as he was Roscoe's pig this would be his costume day and night.

"Well, one thing," vowed Chester, "I'll give this old clown the slip the first chance I get."

Chester's first chance came on the very first train trip. Roscoe hadn't bothered to chain his pet pig; he kept him under the seat with his suitcase, figuring if the pig got loose on the train he wouldn't get far. But Chester figured otherwise; and as the clown was lighting a cigar, he squirted from under the seat and went racing away through the aisle.

Roscoe was surprisingly spry for an old fellow, and halfway down the car the big clown's feet were slapping close at the panicky pig's heels. He would have caught Chester for sure if the tall man hadn't left a long leg in the aisle. Old Roscoe tripped and went sprawling, and by the time he picked himself off the floor the pig had reached the caboose and squeezed his way out the door.

Then, in desperation, Chester leaped off the back platform to go sliding and tumbling over a steep embankment and down into a dense pine forest where he was stopped *ker-whump!* by the broad backside of a bear. The big hairy beast whirled around with a snort of surprise, for he had never seen a pig wearing baby clothes before. But then at the same time, Chester had never seen a big hairy bear before, and for a brief instant they sat blinking at one another.

Then one savage snarl from the bear sent the terrified pig squealing off into the wilderness, plowing headlong through brambles and brush, then frantically leaping the fallen timbers. This time Chester was running for his life, and the bear was close on his trail, eating up the distance in long easy strides. He was only one jump away when all of a sudden . . .

. . . he stopped with a snort and stood up. The pig had run straight for the camp of three tattered old tramps, and the bear wanted no part of them. His last meeting with men had cost him a piece of one ear, so with a grumbling growl he turned and lumbered off.

No wonder the bear was so scared, thought Chester, after taking one look at the three fierce faces overgrown with beards — rusty red, grizzled gray, and bushy black. They were enough to scare anyone.

So Chester decided to take his chances in the woods — but not quite quickly enough. Just as he turned to go, the red beard sprang and in one wild grab seized the flying cape, jerked the pig off his feet, then stuffed him snout-first into a sack.

"Can't leave you out here in the woods, piggy," he muttered as he tied the top of the sack. "It's not safe."

"He's safe enough now," grinned the gray beard. "At least till suppertime."

"Now all we need is beans," said black beard. "Nothing like pork and beans."

"Turnip greens," said gray beard. "They're best with roast pig."

"Oh no," growled red, "he's gonna be boiled with a batch of sauerkraut."

Just then a train whistle echoed through the pines; and the three tramps quickly gathered up their gear, strapped on their packs, and hurried off through the woods toward the railroad, with red beard toting the pig sack.

Although he couldn't see, Chester could tell by the bouncing of the sack and the growing rumble of train wheels just what was happening. The rumbling grew into heavy thunder as the three tramps caught up with the long freight crawling up the steep mountain grade. They scrambled up the ladder to the top of a boxcar, then settled down for a free and easy ride to most anywhere.

It was a miserable trip for Chester. The day was scorching hot, and he was barely able to breathe through the sack. But he was no worse off than the three tramps who rode along under an endless cloud of train smoke which showered them with hot cinders and soot, and in their misery they began to quarrel.

"I'm the one that caught this pig," red beard roared above the noise of the train, "so I'm keepin' him all to myself!"

"Oh no, you don't!" bellowed black beard. "It's share and share alike! That's the rule!"

"And rules is rules," growled gray beard.

"I'm breakin' the rules," roared red, "so what can you do about it?"

And the shouting went on through the long hot smoky afternoon; and at the end of the day when the train pulled into a freight yard on the outskirts of a big city, the quarrel had gone so far the tramps had decided to split up. But before they parted they had one last fight over Chester, a furious tug of war with all three jerking and pulling on the sack at once. Suddenly the sack ripped in two and out popped the pig!

In one bounce Chester was on his feet and bounding away over the tracks across the freight yard straight into the path of a speeding locomotive. Lucky thing that the pig was light on his feet — he hadn't eaten for days — and in one leap he sailed lightly over the cowcatcher, leaving the three beards waiting for the train to pass. By the time the caboose came rattling by, the pig was long gone. He had disappeared into the big city beyond.

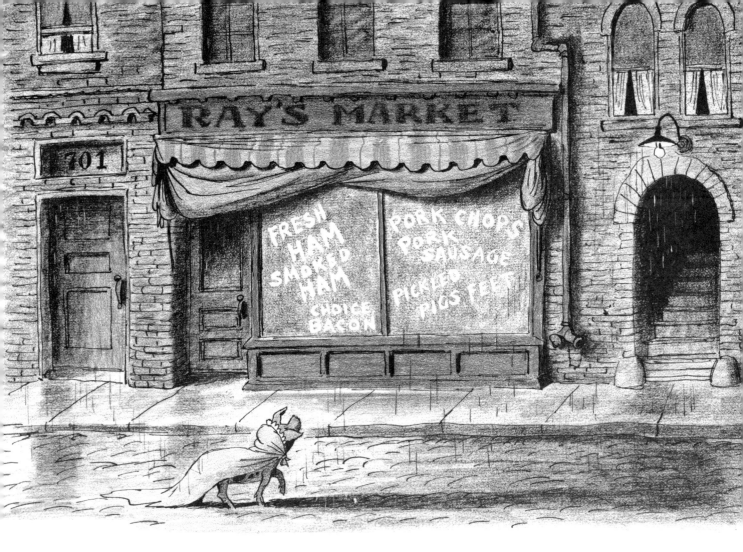

As night came on it began to drizzle, and the bedraggled pig wandered aimlessly along the dreary streets with no idea of where he was going.

On every side were dark ghostly buildings with their yawning doorways and dingy storefronts. And it seemed to the small pig that every other store was a butcher shop with all the signs of doom printed boldly on the windows: FRESH HAM! SMOKED HAM! CHOICE BACON! PORK CHOPS! PORK SAUSAGE! PICKLED PIGS' FEET!

It was plain to see that the big city was no place for a pig, at least a live pig.

"Well, one thing," sighed Chester, "I'm much too tired to figure out anything tonight." And he wandered into a narrow alley where he found an overturned barrel by a junk heap. He crawled in out of the drizzle, and with a groan of despair the unhappy pig dropped off to sleep.

Chester was up and on his way before daylight. He was taking no chances of getting caught in the big city, for now he had made other plans. And he hurried along the deserted streets, always going in the direction which he figured would take him out into the country.

When the sun peeped over the horizon, he was trotting along a dusty road past the wheat fields; then at the first barn lot he came to, he turned in the gate to give himself up, and the farmer greeted the stray pig with open arms.

First the farmer shucked off the bonnet and dress, just in case someone might be out looking for a pig wearing baby clothes, then plunked him in a pen and filled the trough. He intended to make the most of this free little pig, which was just fine with Chester, for he had decided that if he must go the way of all pigs then he was going in a great big way. So he ate his fill every day and, like any other pig, when he wasn't eating he was sleeping.

To the farmer's delight, after a couple of years Chester ballooned into a huge blimp of a pig; and one morning the happy farmer said, "Today this little pig goes to market."

On that very same morning a carnival van stopped at the farm, and out of the cab stepped a dignified white-whiskered man with a broad-brimmed hat and fancy frock coat. He had stopped to buy fresh eggs, but when he saw the huge pig he forgot all about the eggs.

"What will you take for your pig?" he asked. The farmer thought for a minute, then named his price, which was at least twice what he figured the pig was worth. And to the farmer's surprise, the man didn't so much as bat an eye; he counted out the money and the deal was closed.

After the pig was loaded aboard and the van drove away, the farmer had himself a good laugh. "So he thinks he's bought the world's biggest pig! Why I've seen at least a dozen bigger ones at the county fair." But if the fellow had gone to school long enough to study geography, he'd have known that Chester was much more than just plain big.

For the next day Chester was introduced to the crowd in the carnival tent as "THE ONE AND ONLY WORLDLY PIG!"

"Now if you will please move in a little closer," said the white-whiskered man, "you will see the entire map of the world imprinted by nature upon this remarkable creature's enormous hide. On his left side, the continents of North and South America, including the land of Australia, which is down under, of course."

The crowd gasped in amazement, while Chester *oinked* in surprise.

He was just as amazed as anyone.

"But that's only the half of it," said the man, turning the pig around on his revolving platform. "On his right side we find Europe, Africa, and Asia, and, for good measure, even that tiny island of Borneo. So you see, my friends, this amazing pig is truly one of nature's wonders, untouched by inks, paints, stains, or dyes; and to remove all possible doubt, we will now give our worldly wonder a good sound scrubbing."

Then Chester was treated to the first bath in all his life, and he squealed with pleasure; it felt good to be clean. Not spotlessly clean, however. When the foamy suds had been rinsed away, the map came out more plainly than ever, with the oceans a glowing pig pink. Then as the admiring crowd rocked the tent with applause, the delighted pig took a few more worldly turns to show off his spectacular spots. But if he had ever heard that show-offish actors were sometimes called "hams," Chester would have surely been horrified.